For Freddie and Lucía,
whose adventures are
just beginning

Henry Holt and Company, LLC
Publishers since 1866
175 Fifth Avenue
New York, New York 10010
mackids.com

Library of Congress Cataloging-in-Publication Data is available
ISBN 978-0-8050-9901-0

Henry Holt books may be purchased for business or promotional use. For information
on bulk purchases, please contact Macmillan Corporate and Premium Sales Department
at (800) 221-7945 x5442 or by e-mail at specialmarkets@macmillan.com.

First Edition—2014 / Designed by April Ward

Printed in China by Toppan Leefung Printing Ltd., Dongguan City, Guangdong Province
1 3 5 7 9 10 8 6 4 2

And AWAY we GO!

by Migy

HENRY HOLT AND COMPANY

NEW YORK

Special delivery for Mr. Fox!
"Hurray! My balloon is here," said
Mr. Fox. "Now I can fly to the moon.

"Away I go!"

"Wait, Mr. Fox! Can I come too?" asked Elephant.

"Sure you can," said Mr. Fox. "Hop in."

"We might get hungry on our trip," said Elephant.

"Let's bring along some pizza."

"Good idea. Pepperoni, if you please," said Mr. Fox.

"Now away we go!"

"Wait, Mr. Fox," shouted Giraffe.

"Can I come too?"

"Yes—hop in," Mr. Fox said.

"We'll probably get thirsty on our trip," said Giraffe. "Let's pick up some milkshakes."

"Great idea," said Mr. Fox. "Don't forget the straws.

And away we go!"

"Wait, Mr. Fox," cried Squirrel. "Can we come too?"

"Hop right in," Mr. Fox said.

"Let's have some music
on our trip," said Squirrel.

"Wonderful idea," said Mr. Fox.
"Just what we need.

And away we go!"

"Wait, Mr. Fox," bellowed
Rhino. "Can I come too?"

"Jump in," said Mr. Fox. "We have plenty of room."

"If we have music, we'll need some dancing," said Rhino.

"Right you are, Rhino," said Mr. Fox.

"And away we go!"

"Wait, Mr. Fox," yelled some
rabbits. "Can we come too?"
"Come on in," said Mr. Fox.
"The more the merrier."

"We brought our games,"
said the rabbits.
"Let's play," agreed Mr. Fox.

"And away we go!"

"Wait, Mr. Fox," said Bird.

"Can I come too?"

"Join us!" said Mr. Fox.

"Look at our balloon," said Mr. Fox.

"Away it goes!

Oh well, I'll go to the moon another time . . .

"It's much more fun to be here with my friends."